THE BELLY OF THE BEAST

Belly of the Beast

First paperback edition August 2024

Book and cover design by Cara Reents reentsediting@gmail.com

ISBN 978-1-964569-00-0 (paperback)

ISBN 978-1-964569-01-7 (ebook)

Published by Author contact at a.christian.author@gmail.com

To my wife,
who inspires me, challenges me,
anchors me, holds me together, and brings comfort.
None of my work would be possible without your selfless
support.

To my wife,
who inspires me, challenges me,
anchors me, holds me together, and brings comfort.
None of my work would be possible without your steadfast
support.

DEATH

The dust on her face was dry and lifeless. It clung to her sweat and blood as if it was terrified for her. There was a certain poverty about the taste of this dirt. After all, the Almighty Roman Empire had taken so much from this land, even if it did have the Colosseum to show for it.

The ground itself was once that of Roman citizens. Then, a raging fire gave Nero an excellent "Empire" Opportunity. Later, Emperors would return parts of it as a gesture of benevolence. Take it all. Return a portion. Consider it mercy. Then again, it is the Empire.

The limestone had traveled from Tibur. A place five hundred years into the Almighty Roman Empire. That sort of time will make you forget who you were before you were conquered. The limestone brought with it a lurking prophecy of judgment. In the case of this day, arrogance smothered out the voice of caution, warning, or critique. "Who is there to judge us if we are the Almighty Empire?" said the deceptive voice of Arrogance to all Empires across time and geography.

Blood soaked deep into the roots of this place. The legacy of Cain was strong here. Gladiators, slaves, convicts, prisoners. Anyone more profitable dying (or killing) than alive. While crowds may roar for these people, there was an obvious lack of consideration for those down there. Obvious, of course, to an outsider. The unspoken doctrine declared that they had become non-human somewhere along the line.

Animals received and perpetuated abuse just like many carrying the banner of the Empire. Lions, tigers, wolves, bears, leopards, wild boar, elephants, hyenas, buffalo, hippopotamuses, crocodiles, and giraffes. Anything exotic enough to bring a crowd. Anything more profitable dying (or killing) than alive. While crowds may roar for these animals, there was an obvious lack of consideration for those things down there. A misguided, unspoken doctrine that they had earned the privilege to vicariously live out the people's daydreams of violence, domination, and conquest. Of course, it's hard not to daydream in these ways when that fire was first stoked for you before you were born. Then again, it is the Empire.

The crowds did not see this as a worship of violence because, to them, no one worth caring about was getting hurt. They chanted and cheered amongst themselves, against themselves. There was always a particular gurgling when the Colosseum was filling up.

"Come on, Child! It is important to learn about the greatness of our Empire!" a mother shouted.

The child responded eagerly, "Matrona, Matrona, I want to be a GLADIATOR when I grow up!"

"Oh, Child. No, you don't. That's for slaves and prisoners. You have a future ahead of you."

"Marcus, I'll bet fifteen Denarii the Hoplomachus wins today!" an emboldened regular declared.

"So sure of your man's spear work, are you? I'll take you up on that, but your money will just be going right into the brothel behind the stands!" responded the more sober of the two.

"It's going there either way! HA!"

A passerby shouted, "The gods are surely smiling upon us! Quintus, do you remember when that Elephant landed right on top of a gladiator? You won't see something like that beyond the great Roman Colosseum."

"No one tell him about the other entertainment centers and theaters around the world." murmured another man.

The crowds roared and hollered. They saw it more as entertainment. They gobbled it up like the underfed animals they watched tear into people. It was their culture, their atmosphere. In short, it was the All-Roman thing to do. Truly, it was the Roman thing to do. It spoke to the values: Conquer. Dominate. Expand. Now, there was more to Rome than this. There was philosophy. There were ideals of democracy and republic. There were artists, mothers, children, and food. There was humanity. Nevertheless, deep in the ethos, the virus of Empire had infected and, for this time and place, called itself "Roman." The crowds did not see this as a worship of violence, but that's because it looked like almost everything else around them. It was an all-inhaling identity that made a literal spectacle of its so-called adversaries. Worst of all were the adversaries who refused to fight back. Those criminal fiends that would disrespect the honor of Rome on their deathbed. Worst of all were those who robbed the crowd of a good showing by not fearing death nor displaying a violent last performance.

Vita, by the way. Her name is Vita Donum. No one in the Colosseum cared too much to have her name announced or at least remembered. She was far from a glorified gladiator. This was an execution for her and a caution to others. The Lion ripped the flesh from bone and rendered her unrecognizable to anyone who would still see her as human.

"That filthy peasant dog! Good riddance! Long live the Emperor!" The guards were well-experienced in this environment.

"You ought to consider it an honor to have died at the great Colosseum, filthy dog! Long live the Emperor! Death to Rome's enemies!"

The crowd roared.

Centurion Sextus always had a stench of ruthless heckling about him. It fit his role well as part of the Almighty Roman Emperor's army. although his fellow officers often wondered how his reckless language and lashing behavior never managed to get in the way of his status in the Emperor's elite forces. Some blamed his parents; some praised his parents. Regardless, he fitted in well.

The recently promoted Officer Gaius analyzed the centurion's behavior and the carnage on display. In truth, anyone part of the elites would have been just as happy to throw one or two of them in if it kept the crowds roaring inside the Roman Colosseum and the crowds quiet enough outside of it. Bread and games.

"All because she wouldn't deny some nobody criminal? What a pathetic way to die. The misery and stupidity of these delusional, overtaken people."

"Officer Gaius, of course, they'll be ripped apart! They tried to resist the strength of the Empire!" Centurion Sextus said with a twinge of annoyance and an odor of arrogance he had come across honestly.

Sextus always had a certain drunkenness about his demeanor, even when the only spirits he'd consumed were that of strong nationalism and the dehumanization of "the other."

Gaius glanced at the Centurion just as the Emperor spoke up to the Centurions.

"What glory it is of Rome to protect itself from all of the superstitious mules who deny the authority of the Almighty Roman Empire and attempt to stray from our great gods!"

Caseo flinched for a moment. This statement reminded him of his training. All of the unlearning he had to do. He was broken down to less than human and stripped of all identifiers. Then, and only then, was he built back up. Built back up was a strange way to say it, he pondered to himself. Built implies that he became something special, something crafted. Of course, Rome poured more money into the military budgets than anything else (Then again, it's the Empire), but that doesn't mean he wasn't just a commodity to them., property. Of course, he had Roman citizenship and maybe some personal property here or there, but in the end, Caseo's life was owned by the Emperor just as much as the slaves working in the furnace, and his death would matter to the Emperor just as little.

Built back up. Nothing before his training was intended to remain. In short, he was an entirely new thing: detached, severed, ripped from his former self. No familial identity, cultural heritage, personal thought, or sense of independence. He was "a part of something larger than himself." He was part of the Almighty Roman Army. Some things could be assimilated only if they bent the knee to Rome. If anything was to remain, it was because it had benefitted Rome. Then again, it is the Empire.

"The Emperor doesn't own me. He cares about me. Being a Roman soldier is a good thing for me; I have the honor of maintaining peace and order," he said silently as he reassured himself of his assigned place in the world.

The Emperor continued, "Together, we have built this marvelous world for ourselves, and these monsters try to take it away from you. There is no room for them in Rome. No room! If anyone discovers a person who has been indoctrinated into this way of life so contrary and dange…disrespectful to our Empire, let them see our great Empire face to face! In the Colosseum!" The Emperor smelled like death, covered in perfume. Oh, but that perfume was so delightful, so intoxicating.

The entire Colosseum roared with applause. Citizens jumped and hollered, "Long Live Rome" and "Long Live the Emperor!"

"Praise our god, the Emperor! For he is our protection and strength!"

"In the Emperor, we trust!"

"Encore!"

"Again, Again!"

There was no concern for how this dehumanization of "the other" might one day be targeted at one of them. They don't typically like talking about those things.

There again, the Emperor, the Author of Death in this ring, motioned for the next prisoner to be sent in with Vita's still warm blood.

Another young woman. She looked familiar to some of the crowd. Not that long ago, she was considered the daughter of a wealthy civil servant. She was smart and popular. She was an upstanding member of society, at least as much as a daughter was considered to be in Rome. That is until the superstition got her. Some knew her name before this day; afterward, no one could forget her death.

She stepped with grace and mercy. Her integrity caught the crowd off guard. Her dignity was unblemished despite the scene at hand. Despite their best efforts, dehumanization was failing. Perpetua, by the way. Her name is Perpetua.

They let the lion out to collect Perpetua's soul. The Lion stared her down. By this point, it was keen at smelling fear, although there was none to smell here. By this point, it was keen at sensing defensive violence, although there was no intent from

Perpetua. What the lion could smell was invisible to Roman eyes that day. Had it been visible, it would have been putrid. It smelled vulnerability. It sensed meekness. It saw her eyes and said with its own, friend.

Growing impatient, The Emperor motioned for the guard to close in since the lions had not. This was odd but more of a disappointment than anything else. The guard moved in to cut out Perpetua's soul. He stared her down. By this point, he was keen at smelling fear, although there was none to smell here. By this point, he was keen at sensing defensive maneuvers, although there was no intent from Perpetua. Nothing else was noticeable to the soldier until he locked eyes. Her eyes spoke to him. They said, friend. They said, "Do what you must as I have done what I must." Her eyes said, "I forgive you."

He couldn't bring himself to slaughter such grace and peace. Perpetua raised his sword to her own throat as if with compassion in her eyes, saying, "What you are about to do, do it quickly."

The murder of Perpetua was the sign for the lion keepers to move in. The Lion's temporary calmness was a reflection of Perpetua's inner peace. While the crowd began to be tamed, the lion was not. It leaped, still full of the learned hatred, hunger, and compulsion for blood. The jaws of the lion thundered over the face of the lion keeper while the others did what they could to contain the lion. There was no chance for this lion keeper. It would suffer the same fate as Perpetua. No Roman Citizenship or oath to the Empire would rescue him from this "unfortunate incident."

The crowd roared back up in full celebration. The excitement had an encore. Never mind that he wasn't labeled a prisoner; what really mattered was being entertained and fed. Then again, it is the Empire.

In the Colosseum's underside prison room, there lay Perpetua's father. He felt the tremors of trauma and grief and couldn't differentiate them from the vibration of the crowd's roar. Of course, they were different; one was the grieving of Perpetua, and the other was the endorsement of her death. Crying as he held Perpetua's only child, he grieved.

"Why couldn't she just stay in line? Those followers of The Way! They killed my daughter." Then again, it is the Empire. "Those outside rag-tag followers. I hope they all die in the same way so that no one ever has to fall to their superstition again. I... I can't believe it...All my life, I have been a good, upright Roman citizen. I have always voted, attended public meetings, and supported local efforts. I participate in festivals and make offerings to the gods. None of it. None of it could outweigh what my daughter had done. I don't know what happened to her. Was it my fault? I'll protect you, little child. It's a cruel world out there, but I'll protect you from those followers who took your mother from us."

Meanwhile, Caseo's internal moral rattling only stiffened his external solidarity with the Empire. While deep inside, Caseo wondered what this woman may have done. It was frequently and relentlessly smothered and stifled by the beauty and vibrance of all this life had to offer him. He remembered back to his childhood just long enough to snap him into the luxuries of the present. He dreamed of higher career ambitions just long enough to motivate further loyalty to his commands. He was a good soldier. He kept quiet, followed orders, and only expressed his ideas when directly asked. He was just the make of soldier the Emperor wanted in his army and just the opposite kind of personality. Caseo knew he was lucky to be a soldier and not a prisoner.

"What did you think of the show today, Caseo?" asked Sextus

"I–"

"Get me more wine, ya grub."

"Yes, sir."

"Why did you ask him to join us if you have such a disdain for him, Sextus?" Gaius asked with an observant expression.

"Isn't it obvious? I need to get my wine. That little rat won't ever make it past the position of a signifier, but it sure is fun to have him around."

"Of course, sir."

Sextus paused for a moment. Grumbled and cocked his head toward Gaius, who was now standing behind his left shoulder.

"Do you know why you are here, Gaius?"

Before Gaius had an opportunity to answer, Sextus burst out laughing:

"To get the food! On with you, twit!"

Gaius' pride was always present but hardly more than silent. He was in this field for the long haul. He knew there would be bumps in a career like this, but if he kept his head low when necessary, maybe, just maybe, he would live up to his father's legacy.

"Yes sir, on the way."

Gaius brushed shoulders with Caseo on his way to the food. He found both irritation and community in their similarities. It's too bad Gaius had no need for community.

Caseo understood how Gaius felt about him. He understood friendship was a liability and resistance was a one-way ticket to the belly of a lion or some other beast. So he absorbed the hits and tried his best to survive. None of this was incredibly overt or visible to Caseo because, well, it was abundantly familiar. It would have been like pointing out that humans have feet or that Sextus was intoxicated.

MISSION

If you're going to understand advancement in the Emperor's army, you'd need to understand his will, his desires. Ideally, before he does or before it is told to you."

Gaius and Caseo's commanding officer, Sextus, always taught like this in one-on-one sessions. He cared about Caseo in his own bent way, at least a little bit more than all the other eagles racing to the top out there. Sextus saw a little bit of himself in Caseo, but that wasn't always enough for a Roman soldier to like another Roman soldier. In fact, it's a miracle Sextus didn't hate what he saw. As Sextus saw it, the difference between them was that Caseo would never have the stones to slide past his own position. There was more than that, though. He thought Caseo was valuable. Worth an investment because he would return an investment. This was more affection than anyone else had ever shown Caseo, so he gobbled it up. Caseo got scraps of worth; Sextus got control and loyalty.

"Yes, sir, but what does the Emperor want?"

"World domination."

"Sir, isn't that a big reach with how things are back home or on the streets?"

"You can't ever let the hunger die down. If expansion slows down, it would not be good. There is wealth out there. It is our destiny to get it. Besides, you are employed by the Roman Empire, correct?"

"Yes, sir."

"Not those beggars or expendables out there, correct?"

"Correct, sir."

"Good. You don't work for them, and neither does the Empire. Of course, we cooperate with the citizens when we need something from them specifically or in general, and we always play nice with that good old Roman charm, but make no mistake, that's for results." Then again, it is the Empire.

"Yes, sir. I understand, sir… uhm—"

"Spit it out."

"What if the Emperor is wrong?"

Sextus spit out his drink, which rarely happened with his pallet. His drink sprayed across the table the same way Perpetua's blood did at the Colosseum. It was an expensive drink, at least for someone other than Roman elite officers. The amount of top-notch posca that soaked into his polished oak wood table could have fed those "expendables" for two weeks.

"You should have kept that one in. You know, you can be expendable too if you slow the Empire down."

Caseo went cold for a moment. Wounded memories flashed of the stories his parents had told about when Rome first came to their village.

"It's a good thing I like you, Caseo."

Breath returned to his lungs as he remembered his assigned place in the world.

"It would be a good question, too."

The face of raw confusion and that always present hint of fear on Caseo's face said enough.

Sextus responded after a deep, dissatisfied breath.

"It would be a good question if you were, oh, I don't know, a Carthaginian talking about their general, or those rag-tag Britannians or Hispania, Gaul, Achaea, Judea… All of their leaders were wrong. Because, well, they weren't Roman."

"Yes, sir."

"Never suggest the Emperor isn't what he is."

"Of course not, sir. The Emperor is god."

Caseo wondered how many times this proclamation of faith had been made. He had heard this hundreds of different ways, thousands of different times. It was integrated into education, architecture, music, entertainment, resource supply, citizenship, mythology, and history. It was not always explicit, but it was always present. As a Roman, anywhere he looked, he saw the power, the principality, the authority of "The Almighty Rome."

Then again, it is the Empire.

"Good, well, I think that is enough for today. I'll see you just outside the principia tomorrow morning for your briefing. There is a group of expendables that are… not appreciative of their privileges and duties as Roman citizens."

"Yes, sir. The twistedness of some people to not be grateful for the Emperor's generosity."

"Oh, and take Gaius with you."

"Yes, sir."

Caseo lightly trod to find Gaius in his quarters. With each step, he felt the knots grow. Gaius easily became jealous, even if it was a tamed jealousy. Sometimes, these are the most dangerous of Roman Soldiers. Like an eagle patiently circling in the sky, waiting. His nerves were heavier than his armor, and his fear shimmered more than any metal on him. He was an easy target. He knew it. Out on the street, he might have looked like some grand tyrant, but here, he might have been made with the same fiber and flesh as the food they ate. He knew it. Everyone knew it. That's what made Gaius furious when this sort of thing happened.

Knock, knock.

"Gaius, I have a message from Sextus."

"What is it?"

"We have orders to meet with Sextus just outside the principia—"

"—We? What do you mean we? Why wasn't I informed directly?"

"I—"

"—Caseo, you don't know anything! Keep your breath to yourself!"

Gaius' breath caught up to the tempo of his speech. His eyes are darted, arms tensed, legs paced.

"Why does he do this? It's bad enough our centurion meets with you, of all people, one-on-one. It's not like you two have anything in common! You'll never be good enough to stand as his mentee. I hate him! He twists and schemes and probably got the two of us scrambled in his drunken mind."

Gaius's pride and jealousy weren't always silent.

"Are you done?" Caseo said with discomfort

"Tomorrow morning. At dawn. He said something about superstitious or ungrateful people, some cult or something stirring up trouble," Caseo said as he tried to survive his past, present, and future. "I'll meet you there."

"Fuck off," Gaius snapped.

Gaius wasn't especially reckless or a maverick. He just didn't expect much more from Caseo than he did the walls of his quarters in terms of thinking or talking after being yelled at. His perception of Caseo was just like everyone else's. Then again, it is

the Empire. Gaius went to bed that night, like he did most nights, smoldering.

ABANDONED

At ad before dawn, the two soldiers met for orders. Sextus had been a couple of minutes ahead of them with his morning routine of spirits. He still had as crisp and clear an eye as any eagle you've ever seen.

"Boys, good to see your sorry asses this morning."

"I've got a mission for you. Reports show that a group of religious outliers are somewhere in the southeast pastures. They are congregating. I need you two to investigate further."

"The followers of The Way?" Gaius said. "I didn't know they were this close. I had heard about them near Jerusalem."

"They're spreading," grumbled Sextus, "That is why it is critical that you bring back reliable information on their whereabouts and any information on what in the world they are doing."

"Is this the group that worships some preacher we killed a while back?" Caseo asked.

"That's them. A persistent, vicious bunch." Sextus admitted. Almost as a compliment had it not been for the direction he perceived violence being strewn.

"Is it true they are cannibals? Are they really incestuous?" Gaius scraped in so as not to lose relevance in the conversation.

Sextus caught on to it because he uses the same strategy. This time, it irritated him, though. Almost as if Gaius could one day have the capacity to be a rival.

"Well, You're going to let me know after tomorrow." Sextus sternly redirected the conversation.

"We don't want them emboldened and continuing to spread, so we can't scare them off quite yet. Do you both understand?"

"Yes, sir."

"Yes, sir."

As the heels of their horses clicked, they strode through the hills, looking for the Christian community that had caught the attention of Rome. Gaius and Caseo didn't speak much. They focused on the mission at hand. Furthermore, Gaius focused on his missions at hand. More than anything, Gaius longed for legacy. He longed for status. He would never say it or even think it so clearly, but he longed for validation that he was worth something. That his existence mattered. He needed to taste the glory that mattered more to his father than anything else.

Caseo interrupted the silence, which annoyed Gaius as much as anything else Caseo could have done. "Where do youth think the Christians are hiding? Where did they come from?"

"How should I know? Do I look like a Christian to you?"

Caseo smirked as Gaius' armor reflected into his eye.

Gaius was smoldering but calm, unlike the evening before. They rode through the grass, waiting, waiting for their prey.

"Let's go out to the field," said Gaius as the sun continued to rise above their heads. The heat was smoldering. Everything was smoldering. Especially for Gaius. Something between the weight of armor and a vengeful heat made for a dangerous combination that day.

They dismounted and began to walk. Caseo was always a little more withdrawn than Gaius. Gaius was vigilant. He scanned the surroundings, looking for any sign or person or people that might be seen or seen today. He knelt down as Caseo continued to wander. Gaius found a rock the size of a skull. He picked it up with no intention to keep it for long. Caseo looked for his target. Gaius followed his. It was a swift thing. The blow to Caseo's head, that is. Gaius had trained for this type of thing; he realized the writing on the wall the night before.

"Sextus has a favorite, and it's not me," he scolded himself.

Kill or be killed. Broiling over with envy and fury, Gaius launched a near-fatal blow to his comrade. He rose against his comrade and almost killed him. It felt good for a moment. Gaius was clean at his craft and knew what to do from here. He believed Caseo was dead, so he started to position the body, already preparing his lines:

"Sextus, we were separated, and I— Caseo didn't meet back at the first vineyard. I'm not sure where he might be. I assumed he came back on his own…"

Iteration after iteration, Sextus refined his response.

Gaius had a knack for being ambitious, intelligent, and arrogant. Then again, it is the Empire. Gaius was still a beginner in this world, though. For instance, Sextus always sends out multiple scouting parties. Sextus craves competition, especially when he can rest assured he will win regardless. As Gaius covered his tracks and prepared his performance, another party stood just inside the nearby treeline. Too dark to see. Also ambitious for Sextus' approval.

Gaius rushed back to get out of the area. Ready to give a report for Sextus, losing his observant posture along the way as a double dose of arrogance prematurely set in. He still had some time to burn. Might as well look for the Christians.

The other search party didn't get a great look at Gaius. They knew this would be quite an accomplishment if they could just see him. One horse out of the running, extra fodder for theirs. They followed from a distance until they could get closer without raising too much suspicion. The search party had a knack for being ambitious, observant, and arrogant. Then again, it is the Empire. They were still beginners in this world, though. For instance, a young Christian lay barely covered in the field praying. Quietly, softly praying with each grateful breath the young woman had.

When the horizon seemed clear, she stood up, dusting off the dirt and brush from herself. Caseo's situation caught her attention. It was all too familiar. She walked over. Heart thumping, memories racing, hands trembling. She recognized this condition. She recognized this uniform, just not in this way.

VULNERABLE

It was only a few years earlier in a community not all that far from this field. She loved life, and her community did too. It was saturated with joy that flowed from each member. Compassion pumped through this community in a way foreign to any outside of it. Sure, they had fights, but never violently. Sure, they had conflicts, but they asked for forgiveness and never let the hurt linger. It was as if they had larger things to be concerned about. It was also as if these were the most important things in life. How they related to one another was as if they were a family closer than blood and bone. Charis, by the way. Charis was her name.

Charis was on the way home one day after gathering some supplies. She hummed on her way home in the way only someone full of joy can do. No worries or fear in the world. All cares and trust in something. Something as close as breath.

As she got closer to her community, she smelled burning. She saw smoke. She had heard these sorts of stories and, being a wise young woman, knew it could happen to her family one day. She began to run as the tempo of her feet joined in the quick-paced tragedy of her heart. Red. Red everywhere. Red flames. Red blood. Red uniforms. Red banners. Charis' heart sank into the dirt as she saw her entire community slaughtered. It wasn't surprising in terms of possibility. They were a peaceful people with no weapons or means of defense. It was heartbreaking in the way only the meek, vulnerable, brokenhearted sufferers know. She knew their crime. She had shared it with them. During worship and scripture readings. During service and forgiveness. In the way they lived, in the way they shared. They were guilty of a contagious conversion to Christianity that seemed to threaten Rome. For an all-powerful superpower, it seemed to feel threatened easily. Then again, it is the Empire. Charis rushed to find her mother. Her father. Her brother. Her friends. Her neighbors. In life and death, it was hard to distinguish them. In life, they loved one another so freely regardless of familial relationship. In death, they had been beaten beyond recognition. Something about Imperial Security, keeping the peace, or showing the troublemakers their place in a civilized society. Then again, it is the Empire. As the last animals rode out of sight, she looked up, tears flooding and her heart throbbing. She vowed to herself not to let this be the end of their stories or the stories of the Romans who killed them.

Charis stared at the crimson-red stitching of Caseo's uniform now. Is it the work of a thread to become a uniform? Is it the fault of a strand that it becomes frayed or out of place?

Charis instinctually moved toward Caseo's grumbling body. She had been moved with pity for him. His form groaned. His very blood cried out from the ground. Charis knew no medicine but compassion and had no bandage but mercy. This wasn't necessarily a discounted medicine, even in a situation this physically demanding. Her first nature had been mounded on top of over the years. Layers of innocence, love, and mercy. Layers of anger and fury and pain. Layers of peace, humility, compassion, redemption, healing. They swarmed like doves and locusts and seraphim. She looked for a breath. She found it. Both his and hers. She assessed the damage. His helmet had certainly infiltrated his mind. It would be painful to separate them, but with skill, patience, and discernment, it could be done. Charis had seen it done more than one way back at her new community of followers. Sextus had been right; they were a persistent bunch. She began to manage the bleeding as best she could before preparing to pull him out of sight for his own safety. It was only a matter of time before they came back for his metal and leather.

She couldn't carry him alone. The community's home wasn't far away. It always seemed close, accessible. She rushed back to tell some of the community about the situation. Before she finished speaking, they turned her around and followed her to find their new friend, Caseo. They had felt sorry for him and were moved with compassion.

With olive branches and cloth, they made a stretcher. The taint of red was significant, but he was not too far gone. Four friends carefully turned him on his side and laid him back on the stretcher. Caseo moved and grumbled. Not quite conscious, not dead, deep in the struggle. It took time, and the sun beat water out of their foreheads, but eventually, they returned to the community with Caseo in the center of it. They lowered the stretcher the man was lying on.

Caseo still had not opened his eyes. He still had not come alive or awake. Caseo was inside a small hut that they kept well stocked for all of the "travelers," like Caseo, who needed a place to stop for a while. Their journeys were hard. The road can be long and vicious sometimes. Charis and the community knew this all too well. It was humble compared to anything Caseo had stayed in lately, but it was better kept than any of the surrounding houses in the community. Resources seemed to be attracted to the most vulnerable in a community like this. They bandaged his wounds, pouring on oil and wine. He would stay here for at least a few days, being cared for by his new friends and neighbors.

COLLAPSE

The day had ended, and Gaius had perfected his lines. He had prepared and invented them. In fact, he was on his own ambitious journey to giving Sextus orders in his imagination.

"It's a wonder how high we can build when we believe in ourselves."

"I'll take the unit to new heights!" Gaius exclaimed quietly to himself in his quarters.

"And then, when my potential is recognized, I'll take Rome to even higher heights! We will build ourselves so high that we reach to the heavens! I can make a name for myself. Otherwise, we shall be scattered abroad upon the face of the whole earth."

With an abrupt knock on the door and interrogating lean, none other but Sextus lurched into Gaius' dreams.

"Gaius… I've been looking all over for you! Where have you been?"

Sextus was smiling. He never smiled. Even still, this smirk was familiar to Gaius, he had seen it in the mirror just a few moments ago. He had his helmet off, and his rough but polished bald head glared. Everyone imagined that Sextus had lost his hair from the weight of war and killing on previous campaigns. It had never brought Gaius comfort. Now, it gave him something to focus on while he came to grips.

Gaius held his composure but certainly understood the potential for his wit to be outmatched.

Sextus approached. "Where is Caseo?" Cold, quiet, knowing.

"I do not know. Am I Caseo's keeper?" Gaius responded, holding back a smirk. This was modified from his perfected lines; he wasn't as prepared as he had thought.

"What have you done?" growled Sextus.

"My soldier's blood is on your hands, and you have the audacity to disgrace me with your lies?"

"If you wanted to be raised up in Rome, you had an odd way of doing it, boy. I knew your father. He would be disappointed in you."

Gaius hadn't put scales on for that wound today. He assumed no one knew him. Everything created an atmosphere that felt unseen to him. He was being shackled and soon on the way to his cell. His fate finally matched one of his interior composure. Headed for death. Bound by something he couldn't reach the key of. As he stared off into the collapse of his tower of dreams and selfish ambition. A few of Sextus' soldiers clamped his wrists. He half-heard the last bit of narration his former master had to offer.

"You have made yourself an enemy of Rome, and I trust you know the price." Sextus stood up straight, imagining himself the embodiment of justice as he said this. The Empire had a way of doing this. Becoming its own enemy, that is. Trust was scarce. Then again, it is the Empire.

Gaius' former colleagues weren't his colleagues anymore, and their mission hadn't changed. Gaius heard the clanging of their armor and knew they were still just fighting the enemies of the Empire. Sextus was right. Thrown in a cell, stripped of the only shell he'd ever felt home to, Gaius covered his vital organs as if to survive heartbreak with more burial. He tried to scheme, but it was difficult in an enclosed cell with little more than the acquaintance of despair and witnesses only meters away.

He turned to silence, but he had never known silence with the pounding, screeching question of "Worthy?" always trapped between his ears. He tried to feed its raspy, starving voice, and it only got stronger. Besides, that's what got him here in the first place. The little bit of light that shone on Gaius was slowly blotted out by the growing shadow of Sextus.

"I'll see you hang in the morning sun after next you damn fool."

"To think I ever considered you a potential rival," Sextus murmured to himself.

Gaius heard it. Gaius heard it loud and clear. The capital punishment for murdering Caseo? Nevermind that. This was a greater truth than Sextus had ever shared with him before. It simultaneously broke Gaius' hope and accomplished his validation, all in a half-hearted breath that lacked true vulnerability because it was spoken to a dead man. It startled Gaius. If his tower of ambition hadn't already collapsed, he would have been shouting it from the highest level.

His blood ran cold as he realized how far his fall from grace had come. One day, he was two levels up from the Colosseum. He had fallen off the social railing of the Roman Imperial Army. It felt like maybe he was always at the bottom. He felt like he had dropped from the heavens. He had nothing. He felt nothing. As far as he knew, he was nothing. Nothing but scrap and feces excreted from the beast.

MENDING

Caseo opened his eyes for the first time in who knows how long. He had been lying in this bed for days. He had been intoxicated with fear and the siren's call of greater power, or at least survival, for as long as he could remember.

He blinked and blinked again. He saw an old, gentle man tirelessly, joyfully standing above him.

"Good Morning, sir! It's good to see your eyes today!"

Caseo startled and would have jumped off the table where he lay had it not been for a pounding headache, which was fended off by a gentle touch on his arm.

The man had a warm smile to his eyebrows and a look in his eyes Caseo hadn't seen since the last time he saw his mother. It was a consistent smile. The kind of smile that had little to do with whatever the hell and heaven was going on around. A much more stable, warm, deep smile than that. This felt utterly foreign yet strangely inviting to Caseo.

"Where am I?"

"Which garrison is this?"

"Oh! Hehe. Well, Caseo, you're not in a Garrison right now! I don't think I'd be very welcome there. Nonetheless, we will fix you up very shortly. You did incur quite the hit, as Charis said. Some buddy of yours, it seemed. Until, of course, you know."

Joseph's head was hairless. He looked like some kind of ordinary beggar except for the smile on his face and the light in his eyes. He looked like he had seen a few things in his lifetime. Judging by the scars on his revealed scalp, he had more than one incident like Caseo's. While there was something weak and soft about this bald, little man, there seemed to be something sacred and peaceful about his presence too. He was unlike anything Caseo had quite seen. Everyone in the community knew that Joseph had lost his hair from the weight of grief and suffering in previous communities. They all knew this because he was open about it. There was no shame, and suffering was lamented in community here.

"What?"

"Oh, well you… come to think of it, there might be lots to catch up on. Well, let's start here, Caseo. My name is Joseph. I've been praying for and treating your head the past few days."

"Days? Sextus will have me strung up outside base. I must go. Where is Gaius? I was traveling with Gaius." He began to stand up and found himself lightheaded and weak.

"Is that the name of the fellow that launched a stone into the back of your head? He may not be so friendly, Caseo."

"No, he wouldn't do something like… Well, what makes you say that? Who are you? Where am I?"

Charis moved in and quietly and observed the waking soldier, who seemed anxious and ungrateful for starters.

"Oh Caseo! This is Charis! She is the one who found you and told us to come save you before you died out there in the blistering heat a few days ago!"

"It's… nice to meet you, Cas—"

"Where am I? Is this a temple? Who were you praying to?"

"Oh, well, I don't know if you know him…"

Caseo scoffed, "Know him? What is that supposed to mean? I'm a Roman soldier constantly assisting in the maintenance of our society, and that includes temple rounds. Although, I don't know this pl—Where am I? What have you done with my armor?"

"We took it off so you could breathe! I promise it is right over there!" pointing to the corner of the small hut.

"We have no use for such things! You can have it back once you are all healed."

Charis' eyes began to tremble as she glanced at the sword and remembered just how capable such a possession was. She glanced back at Caseo with compassion, wondering which one possessed the other.

Caseo paused, cocked his head toward Joseph again, and asked with fear smothered in curiosity, "Where am I?"

"You… You're in our home," Charis said as she trembled and swept her eyes across the floor.

Caseo paused, breathing in their concern and hesitation. He wondered who might both help a Roman Soldier and be worried about disclosing information to him.

"Who were you praying to?"

GUILTY

The sun was rising on Gaius' last day. These eyes would never see the world after today. Shackles on, Gaius was marched to trial.

"This shouldn't take long," Sextus murmured with resentment in the back of the room with his arms folded.

Gaius looked back, realizing the nightmare was no dream at all.

The prosecuting office stepped forward, thinking that, in another world, this would have been his most clever plan yet. Everything was dull and faded for Gaius. Nothing lined up; nothing mattered. Everything was over, and he only had a couple of formalities left.

"Well, Gaius? Are you guilty?" the military tribunal asked impatiently for the third time.

"Guilty."

"Do you have any answer to these crimes? There are many charges brought against you."

"Guilty."

"Very well. Does anyone see any reason to reconsider capital punishment for the case at hand?"

"No! Boo! Let's wrap this up!" Sextus heckled from the back.

No one crossed Sextus. Mostly because they knew he very well might be capable of the same thing as Gaius, even if it brought him down too.

One officer on the military tribunal had seen Sextus rise over the past few years. He was growing irritated with the arrogance of the stupid runt.

"And what do you wish us to do with this man you cannot get enough of, Sextus?"

The room lightly chuckled at Sextus' expense.

He was smart enough to understand, dumb enough not to know what to say, and arrogant enough to speak anyway.

"Cru-Crucify him! Sir!" Sextus spat out as quickly as he could.

It was a clean-cut case in and out and up. Gaius was dragged out to his cross and strung up with nails in his hands and ropes for "support." Gaius was strong and healthy, even based on the high standard of a Roman soldier, so this death would take awhile. He draped, balancing the pain between his hands, lungs, and feet as much as a tortured soul can in an impossible situation. The morning turned into a hot noonday sun that burnt and battered him from above. Sextus stopped by a few times just to taunt him from below. A few strangers threw rocks at him. So did the soldiers who read his sign. Noonday turned into evening.

It didn't make much of a difference because Gaius' eyes had already drooped shut, and his pain was so unbearable that he would faint any moment. The sky became dark and passersby all found their way home. He opened his eyes to see blood dripping to the base of his cross. He fainted back into nothingness. He woke to the plucking of birds. While shooing off the premature vultures, he saw a man in the middle of the night. The man looked average in most ways. He certainly wasn't Roman. His posture gave that much away even to a dying Gaius.

The man spoke up, "Hello. Peace be with you."

Gaius couldn't believe this. Even at the eleventh hour, hecklers came to him. He murmured back, saying nothing that could be understood.

"I know, Gaius. I know."

Gaius looked at his feet, expecting to see his name on the sign. No one had used it all day, but maybe this stranger could raise the ante.

Gaius stared him down. "What do you want? Why are you here?"

"I came to proclaim good news to the poor. I was sent to proclaim freedom to the prisoners, recovery of sight for the blind, and to set the oppressed free. The more pressing question might be for you, Gaius. What do you want? What can I do for you?"

"Hmph. Nothing. I think I'm all set," Gaius said out of an uncomfortable, seemingly inevitable agreement with fate.

The man moved to the foot of the cross and reached out his hand.

"I know your pain, Gaius. You aren't alone. You've never been alone."

Gaius scoffed as he considered the chances that this was some kind of lunatic.

"You look like a good man. You also don't look like you've ever hung on a cross."

"I am a good man. But you'd be surprised," Jesus said as he rubbed his palms.

Gaius' eye were fixed on the man. Puzzled as he considered the chance that this was some kind of liar.

"Are you?" Jesus said.

"What?"

"Are you a good man, Gaius?"

"Ehm. Let's just say…" Gaius thought to himself. If there ever was a time to be honest to the bones, it was then. No reason to cover for an image or even soothe oneself. It was all wrapped up in a couple pints of blood anyway.

"I'm guilty," Gaius barfed out. "Not just of what got me on the cross, no. It really is true. Live by the sword; die by the sword. Wherever that came from, it's true. Kill or be killed."

"—And it cuts both ways, does it not?" Jesus interjected.

Gaius looked into his eyes. How did such a compassionate man know so much about the wretched? Gaius thought to himself.

"Maybe it's because I care about them. Maybe it's because I care about you, Gaius, son of Marcus and Julia."

"What? How do you know their names?"

Jesus left him a calm silence to process.

"Well, I came to proclaim good news to the poor and freedom to the prisoners, like I told you. But I won't force them. I won't force you. Gaius, what can I do for you?"

Gaius stared as he considered the chances this was some kind of Lord or King.

"Can you help me down? I have nowhere to go and nothing to live for."

The dam was finally cracking. Years of filler and half-measured repairs had anticipated a moment like this. Gaius sobbed. His tears and blood blended as they fell on Jesus' hands, hastily untying his friend.

Gaius looked into his eyes. In that moment, he realized something. Everything he had ever done to try and be worthy had moved him farther from what that meant in the eyes of this man. And then he looked again and realized not even that was true. No matter how long or fast he ran. No matter away from or toward, Gaius was bound to come face to face with this man. It was as if he held Truth and he nurtured life itself. There was no need for all of this man, and yet he loved questions and was patient with invitations. If there ever was a way, it was him.

Gaius couldn't see clearly as he acknowledged a deep physical, soulful brokenness that had long quaked for healing. Gaius let go of all that he had held on to. His body admitted exhaustion; his mind admitted limitation; his heart admitted vulnerability.

"I'm so sorry," Gaius choked as his eyes overflowed.

"Son, your sins are forgiven."

HEALING

aseo woke up with another morning, well, late morning. He regained consciousness here and there. It's hard work healing from the scars life leaves on us. While Caseo expected this to go quickly, Joseph was right there, ready for when it didn't. It had become their morning routine. Caseo would get up. He would fall. Joseph would be there to pick him up and show him back to a place where he could heal. Joseph wasn't a perfect man, but he was kinder and more loving than anyone Caseo had known before the incident. Joseph never had any children or wife of his own. He was rather unliked before meeting the Teacher and his followers.

"Why don't you just let me fall?" Caseo griped in the irritated bark of a young dog.

"It simply is not who I am."

"Who you are? Who cares?" Caseo deflected as if to show that's not what he was really asking.

"Well, you did ask Caseo."

"You're a fool, Joseph."

"I may be, Caseo, but if I am a fool, I think I'm the most confusing, joyful, handsome fool you've ever met!"

Caseo stared at his healer's raised eyebrows, wondering if he was still lying in the sun-scorched field, hallucinating as his body produced some type of fevered dream. Only Joseph could take such a straightforward insult and receive it as a compliment. It was as if he had learned to absorb others' pain and redeem it into an invitational joy.

Joseph picked up the conversation and lobbed it in a new direction. "Caseo, it's time, you know."

"Know what?"

"I'm sorry to keep information from you for so long. We

were concerned about how you might react. If you'd refuse further help. We weren't sure if you could manage on your own."

Caseo noticed Charis and a few others he had briefly met over the past few days entering the home.

"Caseo, we are Christians. We are followers of The Way. I believe you were sent to come look for us the day you were left abandoned."

It was obvious, unless, of course, you couldn't see beyond the tip of your nose or weren't able to think clearly.

Caseo paused in an effort to refute such a bold and dangerous claim. He jumped to Joseph's defense.

"No, you're nothing like Christians. They're cannibals, and I've heard they have sex with their brothers and sisters."

Joseph chuckled. "Ha! Do they now? Is that what they're saying nowadays? Oh, well, I suppose someday we might have a chance to clarify the meaning of communion and brotherhood."

Caseo scanned the growing crowd in the doorway in search of a single sane person to refute Joseph's claim.

Charis reached for Caseo's shoulder. "Lie down, Caseo; you have quite a journey ahead of you to get healed up."

Caseo shrugged her hand away. "Y-you idiot!"

"You could have assumed what I was looking for, and you brought me here endangering your whole community?"

"You were in need, Caseo."

"Don't you have any idea what we do to villages like this? Don't you have any idea what danger there is for the enemies of Rome?"

"I am fully aware of the danger, Caseo."

"We pillage, and we burn. We tear down, and we slaughter. It doesn't matter what the crime is; to stand against Caesar is to stand against god." Caseo began to look into his lap and pull his arms inward as if to protect himself from swings and blows.

"I've seen this myself, Caseo. This isn't my first community. I used to live not far away where the mouth of the river meets the plains and—"

"—And the rocks stick out from the hills." Caseo gasped for breath. He remembered that day. It lived in his nightmares too.

Red. Red everywhere. Red flames. Red blood. Red anger. Red pain. Red shame. Red guilt swelled inside. Poisonous to the veins. Lethal to reject. Caseo's soul constricted as he hid his eyes in shame and began to cry muffled tears for people who knew he was least qualified to mourn in this company. No one held it against him. No one placed him in shackles. In fact, in their listening and seeing, they removed a few shackles that day. Before long, he was vomiting out words one at a time. His heart tightened, his eyes squinted, unable to see anything but dread and pain. Pain inflicted, pain ricocheted.

Charis slowly reached to hold his heavy jaw. He flinched. With slow, firm, gentle hands, she ran after his lonely head with her hand. Like a shepherd with a sheep, she, too, carried the weight of that day alongside Caseo. She looked into his eyes.

"My mother was there."

Caseo flinched and squirmed. Charis gently and firmly found a way to see him.

"My father was there."

Caseo, exhausted and in despair, flinched a little less.

"My brothers and sisters and family and friends were there."

Caseo hung his head and quaked, dry heaving empty sentences left with only implied words. "I-I-I'm so—"

"I forgive you," Charis said as she genuinely stared into the soul of a man locked away in years of his own pain and guilt and shame.

"I forgive you," she said again as she hugged his shoulder with her hand. "They were amazing at forgiving, and I remember them in this way," Charis added, "They would want this for you," Charis persuaded.

Caseo looked at the crowd surrounded by new and old faces. He quickly looked down, sobbing uncontrollably. Barely able to make out the words he had said silently a thousand times starting that dreaded day:

"I'm so sorry."

One by one, the community nodded and formed their sequence.

"I forgive you."
"I forgive you."
"I forgive you."
"I forgive you."
"I forgive you."

Joseph placed his arm around Caseo. "Son, your sins are forgiven."

This outpouring continued for longer than Caseo could manage. Before he knew it, he had been cloaked in a community hug over his broken and healing body. Their strength was meek. Their power was in their vulnerability. The kingdom they were a part of was nothing like the world Caseo knew. The Kingdom they were a part of was really more of a family that was both here, now, and on the way.

Over the next hour or so the community members went back to other parts of their lives. One by one they flowed out to where they would be needed next, coming and going like a breeze. Joseph was the last one to leave Caseo for the night. He had just gone through the routine of reminding Caseo where everything he might need was and where to find him if he needed anything. Caseo felt stronger, so Joseph gave him some space at night.

"Wait, Joseph."

"Oh! Yessir? What might you need? Are your bandages soaking through?"

"I need to know."

"Oh, I see. This is quite different but still important," Joseph said in joyful anticipation. "What is it?"

"Why?" Caseo stammered with a shaking in his eyes and a quivering in his throat.

Joseph smiled with a serene awe. "Because we were first loved, and so now it flows from us. We forgive as we have been forgiven. We are simply vessels like your water cup."

"I don't understand. How?"

"We should talk about the Teacher tomorrow! I think he'll have better answers or, perhaps, better questions for you!"

Caseo looked puzzled. Nothing made sense. The least impossible thing today was that his headache was growing to be insignificant.

Joseph might as well have given him a hug with his joy-lit smile. "Goodnight, Caseo. I'll be back first thing tomorrow!"

"Goodnight, Joseph, and… thank you. Thank you for saving me."

"Oh, that hasn't happened yet!" Joseph said as he winked at Caseo sitting up on the table he had called home the past few days.

Caseo chuckled as he lay down, staring up. His laughter dissolved into a deep curiosity for these people.

"Dear God of these people, I seek your strength and healing touch. Grant me the fortitude to endure this pain, to mend my broken body, and let me return to… well, ehm… to go wherever you would have me go."

Caseo couldn't sleep that night. He was still deep in the struggle, but he felt lighter than he had in years. He decided to pace around the houses for a little while. There was nothing miraculous, which honestly made their joy and wisdom much more astonishing. They had no material possessions to show for their efforts except for the bloodied bandages from the back of Caseo's head.

Caseo paced a little further outside of the community. He found himself fixed on Joseph's words.

Because we were first loved, and so now it flows from us. We forgive as we have been forgiven. We are simply vessels like your water cup.

He repeated these words in his mind over and over again. Churning to them, hoping for them to sink in or maybe consume him altogether. Caseo didn't know what to hope for. He now knew there was such a thing as hope, though. Hope for even the darkest of places.

Caseo looked up. In the distance, he saw two figures moving toward him. One seemed weak, limping, and crutched over on the other man. They were both quite a distance away.

…and so now it flows from us, rang in Caseo's ears.

Caseo's feet started to catch up to his heart. He began moving toward the pair. One foot in front of the other. He stepped on new ground. New ground that wouldn't always be how he expected it to be. If not for the night he would have been close enough to see them now.

"Hello there!" one of them said. "Have you been with my friend Joseph lately?"

"Uh, well, yes. How do you know him?"

Caseo's voice startled the second man. Not that he could prioritize that much with his wounds still aching from a little while ago. He wasn't bleeding anymore, but it was no miraculous recovery. This man needed a community like the one Caseo had spent time with.

"We need to get him to the community that is healing you. It's urgent, Caseo. Can you help me with that?"

Caseo and the second man both stiffened when he said this.

Caseo shook his head as if to remember that wasn't quite the weirdest part of the day and then quickly stammered.

"No, sir, that's not a problem, but who are you both?"

"Ah yes, good question, Caseo. Well, I am Jesus. I'm Joseph's Teacher."

Caseo immediately found his heart racing and his mind chased after it. His eyes fluttered, and he found himself gently tugged out of the struggle. It was serene and restful. It was good. Now and on the way.

"And, well, this is my friend Gaius. I believe you know each other."

DAWN

Familiar feelings ran through Caseo's arteries. Rage, anger, a sense of injustice. The lurching hound of self-preservation growled in his guts. He fumed. He paused, still not responding to Jesus. Still not moving toward or away from supporting this battered man.

New feelings pumped in Caseo's veins and flooded his heart. Yes, Gaius had tried to kill him. But there was much they shared in common. Caseo saw himself in Gaius. Perhaps Gaius could be forgiven just as Caseo had been. Perhaps. Not today, though.

"J-Jesus, they speak highly of you back at that community, so forgive me if I offend. This man is dangerous. He—"

"And you have never been dangerous to your brothers and sisters?"

"I..." Caseo froze, convicted. Forgiveness felt so good to receive. It took quite some practice to give away.

"Caseo, I want you to look at me."

Caseo looked up, past his nose, at a face that could shine even in the darkest of places.

"I did not wish for you to be left in that field. Neither do I wish for Gaius to be left in this one. Will you carry him and yourself to a place of healing?"

His eyes were gently convicting, persuasive because they saw better in you than you cared to see in yourself. They were freeing. They were inviting. They were humble.

Caseo grumbled as he placed himself under Gaius' armpit.

"Thank you, my friend," Jesus said.

"...Thank—" Gaius began.

"—I'm not doing this for you, Gaius. We both are only in this mess because YOU tried to kill me! I'm doing this for this teacher who saved my life."

Jesus chimed in, "If you think this is a mess, I'd love to hear your comments on where you both were before this. I'm sure there is a lot to talk about when we get back to the community."

Gaius and Caseo both pursed their lips. Their mutual need for forgiveness for many of the same things haunted them. There was a startling freedom in being seen by Jesus. It disrupted something lodged deep inside how they saw themselves. It became easier to hold each other when Jesus even just acknowledged the truth of their condition. While they may not yet like the company, they knew they were not in this alone.

The next morning, Gaius and Caseo woke up to the sun shining on them. Joseph was humming and preparing some food as they both lay in the place Caseo had grown accustomed to awakening in. Now and on the way.

"Good morning, friends!" Joseph said.

"You haven't even spoken to him yet," a groggy and defensive Caseo said.

Gaius, clearly in pain, rolled over to look at the wounds on his hands and feet. Instead, he found fresh bandages and a handmade clay water cup next to him. He had no idea what to expect and no energy to expect. He was exhausted from his wounds and would need plenty of time and nurturing to heal. He found himself in a position where, despite all of his learned survival skills, he only had the choice to trust.

Caseo looked at Gaius with disgust. In doing so, he felt disgusted about himself deep down. He couldn't yet speak to it, but he knew part of what disgusted him about what Gaius had done, was what disgusted him about himself. Red anger. Red shame. Red violence. All masked in dark glass towers and arrogance. Then again, it is the Empire.

Joseph looked at Caseo with compassion. He saw himself in Caseo. Joseph used to hold a similar posture. It was heavy. He knew how hard that life was. One of bitterness and self-reliance. Once of survival, scarcity, and fear. A life of little internal stability and anxiety at every turn. Joseph knew it well, and so he was filled with compassion for such a man as Caseo.

"How are you this morning, Caseo?"

"Fine, Joseph. Thanks." Caseo responded, clearly distracted by Gaius' presence.

There was a brief pause while Caseo stared and Joseph prepared.

"You know, he looks kind of like what you did when you first got here, Caseo."

Caseo was horrified. His face turned white. He couldn't have imagined that the secret was out. Other people could see the similarities between the soldier beaten and left for dead and the soldier doing the beating and then later left for dead. Caseo believed he was all alone with this haunting truth.

"What? What do you mean?" Caseo had never seemed more curious in his stay.

Joseph smiled knowingly as he stared at Caseo's armor, still heeped in the corner from when he first arrived. "Oh, you know. He just carries himself with a certain posture."

"What posture? He is limp on the ground with wounds in his hands and feet."

Joseph didn't say anything immediately. He didn't feel he needed to. He took a breath.

"Caseo, my people say a few things."

"I can tell that by now. What do you mean?" snarked Caseo.

"In our scriptures, the teacher you have met references this: 'Live by the sword, die by the sword'"

"Yes, I understand that. Eventually, a soldier is likely to die for his country unless he wins every fight for his entire life. Which is more likely for Roman soldiers than you might think, Joseph."

"It goes deeper than that, Caseo. The sword cuts both ways every time."

Caseo paused with nothing he knew to say. This was new territory to him.

"Taking someone's life takes a part of you away too. I think you know that better than I do, Caseo."

Caseo paused, trying to get back to where he wanted to be. Anywhere but here. Anywhere but those memories.

Joseph caught him before he hit freefall in his mind. "Our teacher is a healer too. A better one than I am."

Caseo was tired of all of this talk; he was growing irritated and had had enough of his past.

"You people are ridiculous! You bring me in, who, for all you know, could have killed you. And then Gaius, who definitely will try to kill you! All he cares about is promotion and achievement! Accomplishment! The next rank! Why do you people want to die so badly, Joseph?"

"We don't. Anyone who does might not understand the gift the Lord has given them."

"Then why?"

"We don't want to die. But if given only the options of dying with our Lord or living within the beast, we will hesitantly, reluctantly choose to be with our Lord. We love life. Our Lord calls himself the life. But, life is not to be idolized."

"What?"

"It is simply who we are, Caseo. We are called to love, serve, heal, and mend. The Lord makes us vessels, and we pour ointment and seeds of the Kingdom everywhere we go. The movement is larger than any one of us. Any group of us. And so, quite certainly, the Kingdom is here and on its way."

Caseo stared at Gaius, annoyed that he was saved by such a zealous lunatic. The thought didn't come to him that no one else would have considered saving him that day. Nor been an outcast so far from the city. Rome's arrogance, short-sightedness, and pride still had some amount of hold on Caseo. Then again, it is the Empire.

Joseph responded to the silence, "Nevertheless, the sun is rising today. We are only just beginning."

SANCTUARY

Voices earnestly sang. The worship service began in this little community's humble home. Songs of praise and serenity echoed in the hearts of these people as they almost seemed nourished by these experiences. It was as if, in some small way, they anticipated a transformation of the world around them. Not in some hocus pocus way. Not in a clean and tidy way. In a way that would touch the lives of the weak, the homeless, and the vulnerable. They anticipated this because it came from a homeless rabbi more concerned about prostitutes, tax collectors, and outsiders than dogma, doctrine, or societal conventions used to forget about inconvenient people.

"...you, Therefore, have no excuse, you who pass judgment on someone else, for whatever point you judge another, you are condemning yourself because you who pass judgment do the same things..."

"What is this?" Gaius asked, turning to Joseph.

Cheerfully, patiently, yet full of anticipation, Josep said, "It's one of my favorites!"

"It's a letter we got a while back. There's always something to learn from it."

Gaius looked half confused, half defeated. If Joseph still was learning, how would Gaius ever manage to catch on to this life? It seemed there was no finish line, no accomplishment, and certainly no reward or salute from the Emperor for this sort of thing. But, sometimes, this was a world where priceless things just take time, trust, and open hands.

COMMUNITY

eeks passed, days set.

The boys became men.

The immaturity of violence was deeply ingrained in Caseo and Gaius. In some ways, it was a mark of the Beast. It stood in the legacies of Cain, Babylon, the Destroyer, and the Adversary. It tried its damndest to resist the Creator of all good things. It recruited its victims and acted the part of a redeemer despite being antithetical to the one who said, "Blessed are the Peacemakers."

"So, where were you from?" Gaius asked Caseo while bouncing his knee.

The phrase startled Caseo enough to dislodge his fierce daydreaming and mental wrestling.

"What do you mean?" Caseo said, half curious, half defensive.

"Well, I just realized I-I know very little about you, and… Never mind, it was a stupid question anyway," Gaius crossed his arms and looked away, holding back a sigh.

Joseph observed the reaction with knowing eyes and a disarming presence; he chimed in, "That's not a stupid question, Gaius. I was wondering that too and forgot to ask. Where are you from, Caseo?"

Caseo let out a deep sigh before he accepted or denied the challenge in front of him. The air stood silent and stale while the forming conversation deepened and Caseo accepted the invitation of vulnerability.

Caseo fluttered his eyes, hoping he would lose his train of thought or close the conversation shortly.

"My family was from the Gaul Region." Caseo murmered.

Gaius paused, holding his breath before entering territory that he knew could be sensitive."Weren't the Marcomannic Wars and revolts going on around there?"

Caseo stared him down with the narrow eyes of a survivor. "Revolts are often what they were called, yes. Of course, to me, that was home and home being destroyed. To my entire family, it meant death."

"I'm so sorry to hear that, Caseo," Joseph softened.

Caseo looked at him and took another breath.

"My birth name was Rixios. My parents thought I might be a ruler or leader one day. We grew up celebrating the festivals of harvest, winter and springtime. My sisters and I would help collect the crops and trade sometimes at the market."

"How did you become a soldier?" Gaius asked.

"I didn't become a soldier so much as I was snatched. The revolts got worse, and I guess someone felt it would be best to take preventative measures against these revolts against us. Our entire community was destroyed. Burned to the ground. All the young men they could find were roundup and enlisted. They made it clear to us that we weren't a very competitive bunch, but they would tolerate us as their newest recruits."

"Wait, hadn't Gaul been part of the Empire for two hundred and fifty years?" Gaius murmured, confused.

"Loyalty could only be expected one way after the taxes rose and the uprising started." The words fell from Caseo's lips as his head hung low."I saw what they were capable of that day. I was terrified, so I joined them. I didn't have any other option. I didn't know anything better to do."

Tears swelled and dripped from Caseo's eyes as he began to remember the horror of the day.

"It wasn't long before I did those same things. I couldn't stop. I wasn't in a position to just leave anymore. Before I knew it, Rixios was a stranger to me. Someone I had only hardly known."

Quiet filled the room. There was a release as Caseo spoke. It was as if that secret was lodged inside of him, hampering his ability to breathe, to learn, and to move beyond.

Joseph pursed his lips and as he spoke, he gently touched Caseo's shoulder.

"What would you like us to call you, friend?" he gently

asked.

Caseo paused, confused, " Um, Caseo is fine. I'm just used to that now."

"As you wish," Joseph said, "but I need you to know. That name and its origin don't claim you or define you. The Creator of all things has claimed you and calls you Imago Dei, God's own Image, Very Good."

Weeks passed, days set.

And the conquers became peacemakers.

"What do I do with this now?" Caseo asked, not realizing Charis was watching him watch his armor still in the shadow of the room.

"What do you think?" Charis responded, accidentally startling Caseo.

"Well, It has served its purpose, sort of. Either way, I won't be needing it anymore. It weighs far too much to enjoy wearing."

Charis smirked, "Not to mention, it wasn't as foolproof as it looks."

"Oh, no armor never is Charis. That's the trick to close combat. A good soldier finds their opponent's vulnerabilities and exploits them faster than their own can be sought out. But, to your point, strong will and wit do not always win the day."

"Sometimes the weak are made strong, don't you think?" Charis pondered

"What, through some sort of training or discipline?"

"Perhaps, but I mean that we move into miracles through the fearlessness of vulnerability."

"Now, what sort of sense does that make?"

"Certainly not common sense," Charis said with a smile.

Caseo smiled as he remembered it was this compassionate soul that saved him from death.

"But then again, we are not called to be common by this world's standards. You know, some of the Prophets, including Isaiah, had advice for this sort of situation."

"Oh yeah, what did they say to do with your old armor and swords?"

"He shall judge between the nations and shall arbitrate

for many peoples; they shall beat their swords into plowshares and their spears into pruning hooks; nation shall not lift up sword against nation; neither shall they learn war any more. O house of Jacob, come, let us walk in the light of the LORD!"

Caseo wept tears of relief as he accepted a calling to reform his identity of violence into a cultivator of harvest. Memories of red skies and blood soaked fields reminded him just how much he needed this good news.

"It is in these ways, when we are in solidarity with the weak, acknowledge our vulnerability, and know that we are the blessed weak, that the dignity of meekness and the force of Love shines," Charis said, grateful to be in such a time as this.

Weeks passed, days set.

Cruelty converted to compassion.

"No! Stop! No!" Gaius screamed in the middle of the night. His voice rasped, waking Joseph but not himself.

Groggy and stumbling, Joseph rubbed his eyes as he fumbled toward Gaius.

"Gaius, wake up! Wake up! Everything is okay!"

"No! Stop!" Gaius shouted as he woke up to find Joseph staring at him.

Gaius sighed with relief and shame.

"Bad dream, again?" Joseph asked tenderly.

"Something like that," Gaius said as he sat up and clenched his eyes closed.

"What happened?"

Silence polished Joseph's question. The possibility of levity persuaded Gaius to speak.

"In my dream, Caseo and I were on a mission. I was watching myself, and I jammed a stone in the back of Caseo's head. He fell to the ground, lifeless. I watched myself smirk and turn away like some sort of monster!" he took a breath and continued, "It was so real. It was just like when it happened. Why do you all still show up for me? I'm cruel and dangerous and brash—"

"—Now, Gaius, take a breath. You don't need to earn those, just like our love and forgiveness. It comes from the Father simply because you are beloved."

"I just don't get it." Gaius rested his forehead on his arms crossed over his knees.

"Sometimes I don't either, Gaius, but this much I do know. The reality is, that we are not the things we have done, nor the nightmares we have experienced." The gentle eyes of Joseph punctured Gaius' scales and offered a dose of forgiveness.

"What you did that day was not right. It was hurtful, dangerous, and harmful. But today, we have a new opportunity, one that you have been taking for some time now. A new opportunity to turn toward a new way of being in the world. It won't necessarily fix what you have broken, but it is the way forward."

"Is there really hope for me, Joseph?"

"Faith and hope and love always live on, Gaius."

Weeks passed, days set.

Their hurt became healing.

Gaius' scabs opened again as he carried the wood toward the community. He wanted to forget about the day he hung like a decoration of deterrence and fear. He was ready to feel invincible again, although he knew there was probably something better in store for him than that delusion.

"Doing okay over there?" Charis hollered, having seen him stop and look at his hands.

"Yeah, just stopping for a moment!"

Charis knew by now that Gaius didn't just "stop for a moment" She jogged over to him, pulling a piece of cloth along the way.

"Thank you." Gaius sighed as he looked away from his bleeding hands and Charis' bandage.

"You know, these may heal faster if you rested more?"

"I understand, but then who would get the firewood?"

"Caseo, Philip, Joseph, myself. I'm sure anyone would be willing to."

Gaius closed his lips and moved them as if he were trying to speak words he didn't have.

"I just want to do my part. You all have offered me so much, and I don't deserve any of this. The least I can do is—"

"—Gaius, you know how I feel when you talk that way. It's not up to you to try and square the debts we imagine and create for ourselves! Believe it or not, sometimes the part Creator has for you to play is a light burden and a day of rest!"

"Sabbath, right."

"We see you sneak out to gather supplies on the days you're supposed to be resting."

"I figured." Gaius sighed as he looked at his wrapped hands and all the wood he had gathered tucked under Charis' arm.

"C'mon, there's something for you back at the community."

"What is it?"

"A place to rest. A place to accept scars, vulnerability, and the journey."

"That's too easy!" Gaius heckled and smirked at Charis.

Without missing a moment or turning from her stride, she responded, "How come you haven't been able to do it yet?"

Gaius paused before saying "These make my hands feel much better, thank you."

Weeks passed, days set.

The sense of superiority dissolved and left humble servanthood.

The whole community gathered around the fire one cold evening after eating what little food they had. No one was stuffed, but everyone was satisfied—satisfied most deeply with the presence of a community saturated in Love.

Gaius looked deeply into the fire with squinted eyebrows and tight lips.

"What are you thinking about? You look like I did the first time I saw barley porridge at mealtime." Caseo said with a smirk.

Gaius chuckled and smiled. "Ah yes, quite different from the smoked bacon we were used to."

"Yes, but don't slide from my question, brother! What are you thinking about?"

"Okay, okay, I was just thinking, you know, who really is in charge here? I haven't thought about it much since we first got here because, well, it feels so free, and everyone else seems to have that feeling of freedom too. I just think back to before. It was always incredibly clear who was in charge, who made the decisions, who had the authority."

Charis smiled. It was a peculiar question to her. "I mean, I guess, in a sense, all of us. But it is probably more true to say none of us."

"Yeah, is that all cleared up for you now, Gaius?" Caseo teased playfully.

"Yeah, well, not really."

Joseph piped in, "I suppose we have a lot of shared consensus. It is kind of in our bones to value other's perspectives and respectfully listen. We often discern together."

"That makes sense, but what about an authority? In Rome, there was always someone with the power, and you knew it."

Joseph turned his head, curious about what was appealing about such a thing. "Well, I suppose the scriptures we have are authoritative in that they are central to how we discern where and how God is calling us to live."

The whole community nodded their heads in agreement.

Joseph paused, then said, "The God that those scriptures and stories are about claims to be Love. So in a very real sense, Love is the greatest force here. It's nothing like the Empire."

The whole community smiled softly, each remembering their own moments and memories of the Almighty showing up for them.

"Servanthood is love for others and becoming who we are," Charis said. She continued, "I think one of my greatest joys of this life is that needing nothing from us, God still calls us to participate in the service and transformation that God has for the world. It is a joy that we can participate in this," as the last log refined into embers that would burn through the longest night.

Weeks passed, days set.

Impossibility disproved itself, and faith became a guide to what it really meant to discover.

This, like any good endeavor, takes time. It was a journey.

The amount of time doesn't matter at all. What happens in a place like that matters more than can be revealed through another's eyes. Gaius and Caseo's souls needed to be in a community that healed and transformed. They were seen and seeing others. They became new people. Not in the way they did after Rome's training. Quite the opposite, actually. They became re-membered to themselves and the people around them. They were grafted into a family. Their lives and stories were not severed or ripped."They were not ashamed, afraid, or too proud to tell where they had been.". They were not less than. Their lives, every moment since the beginning, were valued. It was as if they, like everyone, were considered the very image of God. They were a part of something larger than themselves in a quite different way than they had ever experienced. During this time, they began to support each other as well. They would give and serve as they were able, not out of debt but in love. When someone was injured, they helped Joseph tend to their needs. When food needed to be gathered, they cheerfully offered themselves. They had been so deeply nourished and wanted to pass it along. Love began to flow from them.

RETURN

One day, Caseo's arms grew humble as he carried the basket of goods into town. It wasn't often that people from the community went to the town, but they had more than they needed this month and were sure there would be homeless in the area hungry and in need. Caseo and Joseph made their way into the streets, brushing shoulders with strangers who knew the kind of trouble these two could make for their neat-and-tidy, society-city lives. They had schedules, jobs, lines they wouldn't cross, and status, and these outsiders were even more of a bother than the homeless at their feet.

"At least the homeless try to be of this city," the passerby scoffed.

Sextus gathered and tracked enough to know some of the community was headed into town today. This was it. The turning point where preparation became achievement and anticipation became underwhelming pseudo-satisfaction. Sextus' months of stalking would provide a return. He ordered his soldiers to move in on the two men who stumbled around, offering the filth food, water, and clothing.

Sextus watched from an ivory-colored balcony as he intended to see the accomplishment of his mission: clean the streets.

The soldiers made contact with the Christians and roughed them up. Joseph looked disappointed but not surprised or caught off guard. His body was relaxed and grateful. His heartbeat was in step with Caseo's, calming the worry within him. The threat of arrest had nothing that could destabilize this. Though it tried, breathing down his neck

Caseo was still green to this side of the world—not the world of arrests, law and order, but the world of nonviolence, peace, respect, and dignity, even when yours was being threatened. Caseo flailed. He tensed, and his breath cut off. Red everywhere— red fear, red cloth, red worry, red banners, red anger.

Sextus looked. He recognized something. First, he recognized a familiar thrashing. Then, a dead man walking.

"Caseo?" Sextus hollered as he hastily made his way to Rome's newest prisoners. They may not have been trapped by illusion, desires, insecurity, shame, and the fear of social banishment, but these irons they arrested people with were real too.

Caseo looked up into eyes he had never quite seen before. They were Sextus'; that was nothing new. But they looked grateful, heartbroken, and heart-mended. It was as if even Sextus had a sparkle of love, grief, compassion, and gratitude under all that armor.

It didn't last long as Sextus sensed his own weakness showing and patched the scales.

"Take these prisoners to their cells. I'll manage them later." Sextus had covered the spot, but Caseo and Joseph had seen a glimpse—a glimpse of a scared, grieving father figure with worry and relief knotted into an affection for the living, breathing Caseo. He hardly knew the Caseo that stood before him in the street that day, but he was alive—more alive than ever.

Caseo and Joseph sat in the cell together, both sitting piled on the floor. Joseph hummed liturgies gently while Caseo stirred silently and still.

A day passed, and it was clear to the community that something had gone wrong.

"Has this happened before?" Gaius asked, pacing back and forth.

"Well, yes, actually, people end up missing quite often when re-entering the city after some time," Charis said as she took a breath.

"Sometimes, they are recognized; other times, their actions are. They may have just been brought in for questioning."

"You know how Maximinus has been."

Gaius mostly knew the Roman sword by the handle. He did, perhaps better than any of these people, know just how

Maximinus has been. It may be less sharp to know the sword by the handle, but it can still be just as laden.

Gaius softly wandered out of the room, scavenging for Caseo's cocoon-like armor to wear one last time. It lay next to Caseo's plowshare. The armor didn't quite fit—he didn't expect it to. A lot had happened since wearing something like this, now and on the way.

REINTRODUCTION

There was clambering in the hall as Sextus wrestled his way through. The door slammed open, and the room filled with silence. Sextus seized a deep breath, stepped into the room, and motioned for the guards to take a hike.

"I don't get it, Caseo! You had a future here! If you wanted religion, we had that here!" Sextus blurted out, recklessly frantic. His tone tried to stay quiet, but just like a lust for conquest, it grew obnoxiously loud.

This was the closest Sextus ever got to personally caring. It was subtle, but it was the only amount of love Sextus could give because it was the only amount of love Sextus had received. Not necessarily been offered, but received. It was not a love that cared, but controlled.

"You could have gone to the temple once a week or more! There would be a community of like-minded people. We could give you a sense of purpose. Sextus wrung his hands as he paced in the small room. He continued, "They get along very well with the Empire! What has gotten into you? Why?" Sextus asked, his voice low, resigned. "You could still have Pax Romana, Caseo, please. You know, some of the musicians are the best the civilized world has ever seen? If you wanted to, you could volunteer for the common good of our society if that's how you want to spend your time. The architecture is magnificent in our temples. There is so much. There are so many! If one doesn't work for you, just go down the street! It's like the market Caseo! Your options are in abundance! Just don't eat the spoiled fruit! Not to mention, it isn't criminal like this group! What has gotten into you? Why?" Sextus' voice went quiet, "You could still have Pax Romana, Caseo, please."

Caseo didn't say a word at first. He listened. He felt compassion for Sextus. His eyes met him the way he saw someone sick in a hospital who looked to him for support. He was different since the last time Sextus had seen him. He has been grafted into something new. He had grown and been molded into someone fruitful and caring. In short, he was entirely new.

"WHY?" Sextus roared. He looked unhinged. Caught between the impulse of a puppy and the capacity of a wolf. His blood boiled, and veins bulged as he racked his brain at the impossibility that someone would, in their right mind, turn down Pax Romana. Empire "Peace."

Joseph gently covered a cough in the corner of the cell, trying to be as respectful as his existence could be in a place like Rome. Sextus glared at him, still running the calculations of Caseo's absurdity in his mind. It hurts to think about something like this. So much training had gone into allegiance. There were pledges, indulgences, gifts, services, and goods available exclusively from the Empire. And like any lie, to a degree, it was true. The only way to have this sort of luxury, this amount of wealth, waste, and excess, was Empire. To conquer everyone and everything other than the demons that propel you to be the very hench force of destruction. Of course, the propaganda and Empire Identity never really explained the cost. It avoided every possible accountability, validating the unnecessary forcing suffering of those conquered. It made invisible the fact that those conquered would, in a generation or so, be given the wonderful possibility to help perpetuate the very violence first inflicted on them. It also downplayed the symptoms and impacts on its people. It neglected how the possessor of materiality becomes the possessed. It neglected the slow drip poison of fear, violence, and superiority, the foundational values of the Empire. It gave wealth to the highest bidder without discussing how they wiped the blood off it. Then again, it is the Empire.

Caseo took a deep breath, and for the first time, possibly ever in his life, he was gentle enough with himself to have a strong spine. He looked into Sextus' eyes and said nothing. He did not speak a word with his lips. He looked Sextus in the eye, unwavering and unflinching. There was no resentment and no blame for Caseo. He had the courage to see Sextus' humanity. An even more challenging step for Caseo, he had the courage to declare his own dignity as a human alongside Sextus. In a sense, Caseo's compassionate eyes said: "We are brothers, not because we are both Roman, but because we are both human. The Creator's Image." Of course, Sextus didn't speak this language, even when making love to his wife. Intimacy and vulnerability were considered liabilities. He turned away quickly. Having been offered an aqueduct of love but turning it down for the hauntings of mud, blood, and rot.

Uncomfortable with what Caseo was drawing out of him, Sextus retreated in the only way a Roman soldier would, emotionally.

"I just don't understand son, you had so much potential. You could have done so much for yourself and you threw it all away as if it was worthless or some cheap goods at the market that were about to expire."

With this, Caseo's silence was still compassion, but it meant something different to Sextus. It meant disrespect. It meant he, perhaps, did consider the life of Rome and the life of the Empire to be temporary, fleeting, and cheap on the things that mattered, even if it cost much of the things that do matter. Caseo's silence affirmed the writing on the wall for Sextus. The truth was unacceptable to Sextus; he wanted to believe this was some misunderstanding and that Caseo was still "Roman" and not the dreadfully "un-Roman" filth that called themselves "Christians."

Sextus sat in silence for a moment. Rubbing his lips together, he sought to accept this without showing remorse. He scoffed, "Blessed are the poor, right, right. You Christians are delusional." He grimaced as he tried to leave the cell behind despite its lingering impact on his psyche.

LIFE

Gaius' palms were sweaty as he paced through the city streets. They were somewhat familiar, somewhat different. Life had a new tint to it, or perhaps a tint pulled away. The city seemed heavier and more lonely than he remembered. He kept his head low, one hand thumbing the handle of his sword. It made him want to puke. The path behind; the path ahead. He knew the routes; not that much had changed. He just hoped nobody saw a dead man walking.

Gaius missed Joseph. And Caseo too. He thought back to things Joseph had said, even about the very people that had caused him so much pain.

"While I believe the empire is evil I feel quite differently about its citizens. There is hope for them. I believe at their genesis they are actually Very Good."

Gaius never quite understood how Joseph could weave the line between how he saw people and what they did. Then again, it saved his life.

"Gaius, you're going to have to learn to look pain in the eyes. You're going to have to learn to look your own pain in the eyes."

These words had stuck with Gaius for a few weeks now. He had seen so much blood, mostly others', some of his own. The pain was incredibly familiar to him, and yet that almost made it unattainable. It was as if, for Gaius, it was all on the other side of the Subiaco Dams—swelling, engineered to be maintained, only to be let out as needed—which, for Gaius, was hardly ever.

"You've got to learn to listen to silence and things unspoken."

This one irritated the hell out of Gaius as he rambled to Joseph one day about Caseo's coldness.

Joseph's conversations with Gaius about forgiveness were always the most challenging for him. Deep down, Gaius, perhaps like all of us, was drawn to it but didn't consider himself worthy of it. Of course, that doesn't matter in a world where priceless things are given out for free. Now and on the way.

Gaius slowly opened the door to the prison cells.

"What are you doing here?" rasped an irritated prison guard, bothered by his own existence in such a place.

"The Centurion called for this one," Gaius stammered quickly, pointing at Joseph.

Gaius knew he couldn't take them both at once. He couldn't easily take them both separately but at least it might be possible one at a time.

" No one tells me anything down here," the guard murmured as he crossed his arms while his ego deflated.

Joseph and Caseo looked astonished into the face of Gaius. Gaius looked at Caseo with soft eyes. Eyes of compassion and motivation. A reassurance of his return. Caseo nodded while Joseph stood up clunkily yet cheerfully.

The door closed behind them, leaving Caseo with his worries and relief. In some way, he felt, it would all be okay. Not because he was safe, nor because safety would be assured. It was an internal serenity uncompromised by the status of his condition nor the constitution of his well-being. It was as if he was untouchable even with his vulnerability fully intact.

The sun rose the next day, and so did Sextus' fury. It was puffing like a lion and squawking like a vulture. By this point, it was clear to Sextus and the guards that something had gone terribly wrong. A blow to the ego. A prisoner escaped, but it was an insignificant prisoner they knew little about and no questions to ask. No, the real tragedy was a vulnerability. The real tragedy was an escape. The real tragedy was a breach. It threatened in a way that was not tolerable.

Gaius wasn't able to make it back for Caseo. The overnight guards picked up, and there wasn't a gap between the scales. He never left his crouched position outside of the city gates, not even as the sun rose.

In the eerie, restrained, quiet voice, Sextus asked, "Where is the man?"

Caseo watched as the centurion's synthetic patience and sense of self-composure combusted. This wasn't just embarrassing; it could be an occupational hazard for Sextus, a risk to his career. If the men Sextus was in charge of could not manage standing orders, how could his leadership be entrusted?

Fear trembled between Sextus' eyes.

Caseo had nothing for him but a quiet calm. The spell finally broke. Caseo found something he was more than willing to live and die for. It was not Sextus. It was not conquest. It was not Rome. It was not the Empire. It was not survival. A grand vision had subverted all of the imperial domineering that Caseo had gorged on. A grand vision that could not be stopped, could not be controlled, could not be commodified, could not be truncated, could not be contained. A grand vision that unapologetically declared that the lives of the little people matter. God sees Hagar. God favors the runt. God finds his home in the backcountry, poor, traveling, and forgotten womb of Mary. God proclaims liberty to the captives, regardless of their prison. God proclaims sight to the blind, regardless of their invisibilities. God proclaims good news to the poor, and that does not mean mammon nor the illusion of power or wealth through purchasing capacities. Now and on the way.

Caseo calmly stared at Sextus. His mind reflected, his heart stirred, his soul transformed. The room was quiet and soft for Caseo. The irritated Sextus seemed strangely irrelevant given a peace untouchable.

"CASEO! Give me a story! I'll give you whatever you may want! What has happened to the man you were with?"

"You think twenty or thirty silver coins can purchase a friendship from me?" Caseo snapped, unafraid to show his disgust for Sextus' implication.

It caught Sextus off guard.

"The truth is, Sextus, that naked I came from my mother's womb, and naked I shall depart. Just like you, my brother."

Now broiling over, Sextus resorted to the physical threats

that typically worked on Caseo. Threats like this hadn't been on Caseo's mind for some time.

"You know, they have a place for people like you at the Colosseum."

"If I perish, I perish," Caseo claimed, fully content with whatever his life may bring.

"So be it," Sextus snarled. Irritated and empty-handed, Sextus moved toward the door. With one hand gripping the frame, he turned back and looked at Caseo's chest.

"What will your composure look like when you are face-to-face with the force of the Empire?"

When it became safe to walk around, playing the part of his former self, Gaius entered the belly of the city, looking for any trace of Caseo. He felt like a stranger in a strange land walking through the street corners and market squares. Caseo was nowhere to be found. It was loud and bustling. No one would rest in the middle of the day like this. Criers announced the Colosseum starting shortly.

Gaius' blood ran cold. It was uncommon. Public Colosseum executions took time, and Maximinus preferred piling the bodies of Christians in pits outside of the city. He couldn't know for sure, but something drew him to follow the swelling crowds.

At this point, the Colosseum repulsed Gaius. He had found a deep sense of compassion for all his fellow human beings. Neither violence nor blood seemed to cultivate much of the world he hoped for anymore. Nevertheless, he drew closer. He needed to know.

Caseo felt the damp stench of violence in his new room he had been moved to. He felt a growing rumble, although it didn't bother him how he had imagined it might. He had found closure in a way no thinker seems to. It was as if he had found clarity in a way the restless and ambitious lack. It was a submission, not to Rome nor to fate, but to give in life and death the gift of love, joy, peace, patience, kindness, goodness, faithfulness, gentleness, and self-control. He was becoming. He was preparing to model something authentic in life and death that the Empire could not understand. It would seem like an illusion or a trick. Maybe even a delusion that had, ironically, captured and possessed another poor victim of "superstition." That's at least what Sextus would say.

There was a taste of poverty. A poverty given away. It was delightful because he had followed orders, but it was more than that. It was calling for Caseo. He looked up to see the royal blue sky above the colosseum.

"Lord, I do not want to die, especially not like this. Life with loved ones and this good world is a gift. But if I must, let it not have the last word."

Caseo raised his head, unfolded his hands, and took a full, peaceful breath. Now and on the way.

The crowds roared.

The door opened.

When a door like this door opens, there are countless possibilities for something to happen. Something to shift. Someone to be transformed.

EPILOGUE

*"If any man has ears to hear, let him
hear."-Jesus Christ (Mark 4:23 KJV)*

"How did we get here?" said the man to his friend.
"I'm not certain, but I have a feeling we've been here
longer than we know."

The two friends moved inside the belly of the vulture.
It was a vessel of decay, and yet something seemed very alive
about it. The men were hungry. They had just woken from a
long, deep sleep. They began to move. They felt the beast's pulse
everywhere they walked. It's mucous drained by their feet. Its
breath brushed past their neck, back and forth. Back and forth. Its
gurgles surrounded them now that they were awake to its sound.
They were looking for a way out, but they could hardly see and
felt everything pressing in. It is easy to lose the light and the hope
in a place like the belly of the beast, but Light is never far away.
No torch was needed to light the way. Tongues of fire that rested
on each of them were enough. The way showed itself. It was true;
life was not going to leave them alone to be part of the beast. They
were tempted to consume something, anything from the beast's
flesh. They guarded each other. They protected each other in
weaker moments. They found light in the midst of heavy darkness.
Clarity in the midst of chaos.

"Don't eat the beast."

"Don't consume its food nor its flesh."

"In either, you will become the very thing it is."

So they did their best to resist what surrounded them.

Their Teacher, a lifelong friend, had gifted each of them
a sword like no other sword. They pulled their swords from their
mouths and used them to perform surgery from within. These were

sharp swords, sharp enough to cut down the nations. They used their swords for precisely that. The two friends joined together, cutting with the hands of surgeons out of the belly of the beast. The length of the process tested them. Their bones held them together. Their tongues of flame intuitively guided them. Many times, they cried, "How long? How long?" Eventually, the way appeared to them. They withdrew from the belly of the beast, and it crumbled. Decreation of the beast began. Behold, the Teacher continued to do a new thing.

"Behold, I am the Living One," said the Teacher.

I thank God for my editor, Cara Reents.

You helped me reconsider the smudges and holes I had long seen as invisible.

Thank you for making this vision legible with me.

NOTE FROM THE AUTHOR

"So, what will you do?"

This book is not exclusively about ancient Rome. Even when it is about "Rome," it is not about Rome per se, but when Rome was infected by the virus of "Beast." This book is about being inside the "Beast," no matter what it is called for that time and place. For me, the Beast is The Almighty United States of America. It is also The Russian Federation. It is also the People's Republic of China. It may also be the mobs in neighborhoods and the manipulation in households. There are more. Some are rising. Some are falling. All will crumble. For you, it may be another.

I believe the Beast is no Christian at all. It has never truly considered itself "under God" but delusionally considers it to be equal to God, among a vague, agnostic "mighty God" that has little in common with the historical Jesus, the Jesus of the Bible. To that point, I believe enslavement is heresy. Jim Crow is heresy. The genocide of indigenous people is heresy. Holding back generations of immigrants and suppressing generations of vulnerable people is heresy. Manifest destiny is heresy. Mass incarceration is heresy. Systematic apathy toward the poor is heresy. All of this is right on course for what John of Patmos calls the beast. Imperialism, as if "us" is the chosen one, is heresy. Violence is heresy. Our Image of God is bruised and beaten by our own hands when we see ourselves as the saviors of other people and the world in this sort of way. This is especially potent when we have a hand or a dollar in their oppression.

I am an Eagle Scout. I've lived in the United States my whole life. I love the people. I have lived with quite expansive privilege and luxury in my life, in part because of the very systems I am speaking to. I may be considered critical, but that is because I love the people within this country. I also love the people outside of this country. I admire the best of the ideals this country has, even if it has not yet been brought to fulfillment. There is a long

way between saying something and it being true. The Snake in the Garden shows us that.

I do not write this as an enemy. Even if I had, my King instructs me to love my enemies. I write this as a concerned friend. I write this as an angry brother who knows there can be better for those who accept Love. Like a friend seeing the self-destructive habits of another, I mourn the bully's pain in the hardened, intoxicated, greedy, ambitious, insecure, spiritually unstable, morally bankrupt, self-destructive virus of the beast.

There used to be a day that if you asked me if the beast was redeemable, I would have lamented the answer "no." Seeing the rise and fall of Babylon and Rome, I imagined its fate sealed.

But my mind has been changed. Even while the conscience of a nation, organization, or person is on hospice and the ghost of Christmas past is visiting, God does indeed still work miracles. The challenge is that God commands participation and repentance.

A reckless parachuter
flailing in the air,
in the mystery of free fall.

Time feels abundant
but must be used intentionally
in order to avoid catastrophe.

We need to learn that our burdens are each others'.

Pray Often, Love Always.

A. Christian